OCT - - 2023

Twice as Many Friends

¡El doble de amigos!

words and music by **Brian Amador**

art by
Vanina Starkoff

Sung by
Sol y Canto

Barefoot Books
Step inside a story

Sometimes
with my family I travel
to places far away.

It always makes me happy
to understand what
people say.

If they say ¿Cómo te llamas?
It means **What's your name?**

If they say ¿Quieres jugar?
It means **Do you want to play?**

If they say ¿Cómo estás?
It means **How do you do?**

And if they say ¡Te quiero!
It means **I love you!**

Twice as many friends,
twice as much fun!
That's why two languages
are better than one!

Sometimes people come to live here
from places far away.

It always makes me happy
to help them know
just what to say.

If they say ¿Cómo te llamas?
It means **What's your name?**

If they say **¿Quieres jugar?**
It means **Do you want to play?**

If they say ¿Cómo estás?
It means How do you do?

And if they say ¡Te quiero!
It means **I love you!**

Twice as many friends,
twice as much fun!
That's why two languages
are better than one!

Me gusta tu estilo
means **I like your style.**

Me gusta tu sonrisa means **I like your smile.**

Lápiz is **pencil**
and **pluma** is **pen**.

¿Serás mi amiga? **Will you be my friend?**

¡El doble de amigos!*
Twice as many friends!
* el DOH-ble de ah-MEE-gohs

¿Cómo te llamas?*
What's your name?
* KOH-moh teh YAH-mahs

¿Quieres jugar?*
Do you want to play?
* KYEH-res hoo-GAR

¿Cómo estás?*
How do you do?
* KOH-moh es-TAHS

¡Te quiero!*
I love you!
* teh KYEH-roh

Me gusta tu estilo.*
I like your style.
* meh GOOS-tah too es-TEE-loh

Me gusta tu sonrisa.*
I like your smile.
* meh GOOS-tah too sohn-RREE-sah

Lápiz*
Pencil
* LAH-peace

Pluma*
Pen
* PLOO-mah

¿Serás mi amiga?*
Will you be my friend?
* se-RAHS mee ah-MEE-gah

Spanish speakers live all over the world. Did you know that the same language can also be spoken in different ways, depending on its location? This is called a **dialect**. For example, in Latin America the Spanish word for "pen" is "pluma." But in Spain, the Spanish word for "pen" is "bolígrafo."

Twice as Many Friends ♥ ¡El doble de amigos!

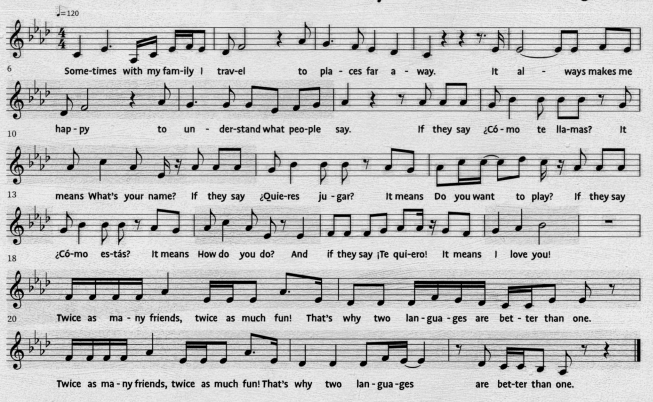

(Lyrics, ♩=120, 4/4)

Some-times with my fam-i-ly I trav-el to pla-ces far a-way. It al-ways makes me hap-py to un-der-stand what peo-ple say. If they say ¿Có-mo te lla-mas? It means What's your name? If they say ¿Quie-res ju-gar? It means Do you want to play? If they say ¿Có-mo es-tás? It means How do you do? And if they say ¡Te qui-ero! It means I love you! Twice as ma-ny friends, twice as much fun! That's why two lan-gua-ges are bet-ter than one. Twice as ma-ny friends, twice as much fun! That's why two lan-gua-ges are bet-ter than one.

To my children Zia and Alisa; and to their mami Rosi, who helped me raise them to be bilingual (and to have twice as many friends!)
— B. A.

For all my friends, in all languages
— V. S.

Barefoot Books would like to thank María-Verónica A. Barnes, Director of Diversity Education at Lexington Montessori School, for her expert input as we developed this book.

Barefoot Books
23 Bradford Street, 2nd Floor
Concord, MA 01742

Barefoot Books
29/30 Fitzroy Square
London, W1T 6LQ

First published in the United States of America by Barefoot Books, Inc
and in Great Britain by Barefoot Books, Ltd in 2023
All rights reserved

Hardback ISBN 978-1-64686-845-2
Paperback ISBN 978-1-64686-846-9
E-book ISBN 978-1-64686-866-7

Text copyright © 2023 by Brian Amador
Illustrations copyright © 2023 by Vanina Starkoff
The moral rights of Brian Amador and
Vanina Starkoff have been asserted

Graphic design by Sarah Soldano, Barefoot Books
Edited and art directed by Emma Parkin and
Bree Reyes, Barefoot Books
Reproduction by Bright Arts, Hong Kong. Printed in China
This book was typeset in Caveat Brush, Duper
and Lonely Hearts Club
The illustrations were prepared in acrylics and finished digitally

British Cataloguing-in-Publication Data: a catalogue record
for this book is available from the British Library

Library of Congress Cataloging-in-Publication Data
is available under LCCN 2022947624

1 3 5 7 9 8 6 4 2

Sung by Sol y Canto
Musical arrangement ℗ 2023 by Brian Amador, Greñudo Music (BMI)
Produced, mixed and mastered by Sol y Canto, Boston, USA
Animation by Collaborate Agency, UK

Go to www.barefootbooks.com/friendsamigos to access your audio singalong and video animation online.

Barefoot Books
Step inside a story

At Barefoot Books, we celebrate art and story that opens the hearts and minds of children from all walks of life, focusing on themes that encourage independence of spirit, enthusiasm for learning and respect for the world's diversity. The welfare of our children is dependent on the welfare of the planet, so we source paper from sustainably managed forests and constantly strive to reduce our environmental impact. Playful, beautiful and created to last a lifetime, our products combine the best of the present with the best of the past to educate our children as the caretakers of tomorrow.

www.barefootbooks.com

Brian Amador is a guitarist, composer, songwriter, singer and voice actor originally from Albuquerque, New Mexico, USA and now residing in the Boston, Massachusetts, USA area. Brian grew up and raised his family in a bilingual household. He has written countless songs for adults and children of all ages – in Spanish, English and both languages combined. Brian and his wife, Rosi are the proud parents of adult twins and a scruffy little dog.

Sol y Canto is the award-winning Pan-Latin ensemble led by Puerto Rican/Argentine singer and percussionist Rosi Amador and New Mexican guitarist and composer Brian Amador. Featuring Rosi's crystalline voice and Brian's lush Spanish guitar and inventive compositions, Sol y Canto is known for making their music accessible to Spanish- and English-speaking audiences of all ages.

Vanina Starkoff was born in Buenos Aires, Argentina and now lives in Buzios, Brazil. She studied graphic design at the University of Buenos Aires and went on to illustrate her first picture book in 2010. Since then, Vanina has gained international recognition for her vivid landscape illustrations, including the critically acclaimed *From My Window*, also published by Barefoot Books.